Bank Street Ready-to-Read™

The Town Mouse
and the Country Mouse

Retold by Ellen Schecter
Illustrated by Holly Hannon

A Byron Preiss Book

BANTAM BOOKS
NEW YORK • TORONTO • LONDON • SYDNEY • AUCKLAND

At the edge of the meadow
in a chink in the wall
by the side of a small country lane
lived a fine Country Mouse.

Her house was small but snug.
She worked hard to fill her cupboards
with dried berries and jam,
wheat cakes and barley corn.

6

The busy Country Mouse stored
sweet silver rain in a hollow rock.
She made bowls and cups from acorns,
and swept her floor
with a homemade broom.
She wove curtains of spider-silk
and rugs of willow wand.
She slept beneath a quilt of rose petals
stitched neatly together with cobweb.

One Fall day, after the Country Mouse
gathered in her harvest, she invited
her cousin who lived in town
to come and visit her.

"I have so much fun here and
have such good things to eat,"
she wrote the Town Mouse.
"Will you please come
share them with me?"

And before a spider could spin a bridge
from here to there,
the Town Mouse tap-tapped
on her country cousin's door.
They greeted each other
with hugs and squeaks.

The Country Mouse welcomed
the Town Mouse like a queen.
She gave her the best seat in the house.
She served toasted oat cakes and
steaming bowls of barley soup.

And for dessert?
One fresh blackberry each,
washed down with rose-bud tea
and a golden drop of clover honey.

The Town Mouse tapped her tiny toes
on the willow-wand rug.
"It's awfully quiet here,"
she complained to her country cousin.
"Isn't there anything to *do*?"

"Let's pick berries,"
suggested the Country Mouse.
"Then we'll climb to the top
of the highest hill."
The Town Mouse wrinkled her pink nose
but tied on a sunbonnet anyway.

It was hot, hard work.
Soon the Town Mouse itched all over
from bug bites and brambles.
She felt forty new freckles
pop out on her nose.

But her country cousin
just hummed happily
along with the bees.

Just as the Town Mouse
sank down on a rock to rest,
dark clouds blew across the sun.
"Look! A storm,"
cheered the Country Mouse.
"Let's race it home!"

18

But the storm was much faster
than they were.
Soon they were soaked to the fur.

The Country Mouse didn't care.
She danced in puddles
and caught raindrops on her tongue.

The Town Mouse tried her best
to run between the raindrops.
But she tripped on a twig,
slipped in the mud,
and landed on her nose.
What a muddy mess!

By the time they reached home,
the rain had stopped.
The Country Mouse bundled up
her cousin and lit a fire.
Night fell and crickets sang.

The Country Mouse opened her curtains
to the moonlight.
She invited the fireflies to perch
and gossip in her lanterns.

The Town Mouse tried to hide
big yawns behind her little paws.
"I miss my dazzle and dancing,"
she said with a sigh.
"I miss my parties and prancing."

Two yawns later, the Country Mouse tucked
her town cousin under the rose petal quilt
and shooed the fireflies into the night.

Next morning, by first light,
the Town Mouse was packed and ready to go.
"I must get back to my hustle and bustle,"
she told her country cousin.

"Won't you come with me?
Tonight we'll dine on cheese and cake.
Tonight we'll dance till dawn in the square.
And, oh, the sights we'll see!"

And, oh, what wonders awaited them
in the big, bright, bustling town.
The Country Mouse's eyes, ears, and nose
had never been so busy!
She saw dancing in the streets,
and shops bursting with wonderful things.

She smelled the warm brown smells
of chocolates and cakes,
and the golden scent of buttered popcorn.
She saw a juggler and a puppet show.

And through all the merry hustle-bustle, she heard a brass band playing *oom-pah-pah* under the stars. But suddenly—

"Watch out!" cried the Town Mouse
as the thundering wheels of a wagon
rushed toward them.

Just in time, she pulled her country cousin
safely out of the way.
The huge wheels missed them by
just the width of their whiskers!

Then the Town Mouse tugged
the Country Mouse gently by the paw.
She led her to a grand town house
with windows that sparkled like diamonds
and a chimney that poked the sky.
At the door stood a huge, hairy watch dog
with a mouth as big as a cave.

As soon as the dog looked away,
the Town Mouse pulled
her country cousin
inside to safety.

"Shhh!" warned the Town Mouse,
leading the way on tiptoe.
Her cousin grabbed her tail and held tight.
She saw lamps as bright as the sun,
dripping glass raindrops that
tinkled when they swayed.
And what were those delicious smells?
She licked her pretty pink lips.

But what was that?
Suddenly, the mice heard big boots
stomping on the stairs.
Something heavy bumped and crashed
above their heads.

Just in time, they ducked under
two big oak doors.
"And now for our feast!"
said the Town Mouse as if
nothing had happened.

The Town Mouse led her trembling
country cousin across a vast dining room.
They climbed up the golden table,
and found themselves on a sea of lace.
And, oh, the treats spread before them!
Chocolate cake and roast beef
on silver platters and sparkling plates!

Jam as red as rubies!
A bread as big as a bed!
A cheese as big as a mouse's house!
The Country Mouse was just about
to take her first scrumptious bite when—

M-M-M-M-R-R-R-E-O-W!
A fat orange cat leaped on the table,
all teeth and claws.
He caught the Country Mouse by her tail.
His mouth opened wide,
full of jagged yellow teeth.
Too scared to squeak,
the Country Mouse pulled her tail free
and jumped right off the table!

"Quick! Follow me!"
squeaked the Town Mouse,
squeezing into a tiny hole by the hearth.

But the Country Mouse started running.
She ran through the grand house...

and down the high steps...

and through the town . . .

and didn't stop running
till she reached her own safe, snug home . . .

and jumped under her own rose petal quilt.

45

And from that day on,
the Town Mouse danced in the dazzle
of her big, bright, bustling streets.

The Country Mouse greeted
each sunrise and sunset
from her own quiet country lane.

And they each knew
exactly where they belonged.

Ellen Schecter writes books, television, and video for children, families, and teachers. Her television credits include two series for Nickelodeon; *Miracle at Moreaux*, a holiday special for the *PBS WONDER-WORKS* series; and many episodes for the Emmy Award-winning PBS *READING RAINBOW* series. Her other books in the BANK STREET READY-TO-READ series include *The Warrior Maiden, Sim Chung and the River Dragon, The Flower of Sheba* (with Doris Orgel), *Diamonds and Toads,* and *Sleep Tight, Pete.* She is Director of Publications and Media at The Bank Street College of Education, and lives exactly where she belongs with her husband and two children in New York City.

Holly Hannon graduated from the Ringling School of Art and Design in 1985 and has since illustrated 14 books for young children, including *The Wind in the Willows, The Jungle Book,* and *The Mouse Who Wanted to Marry.* Ms. Hannon lives exactly where she belongs in Greenville, South Carolina, minutes away from the Blue Ridge Mountains.